D1449012

DISASTER ISLAND

BARTLETT BROTHERS
DISASTER ISLAND
ROGER ELWOOD

WORD
Kids!

WORD PUBLISHING
Dallas·London·Vancouver·Melbourne

DISASTER ISLAND

Copyright © 1992 by Roger Elwood.

All rights reserved. No portion of this book may be reproduced in any form without written permission from the publisher, except for brief quotations in reviews.

Editor: Beverly Phillips

Library of Congress Cataloging-in-Publication Data

Elwood, Roger.
    Disaster island / Roger Elwood.
       p. 2   cm.—(Bartlett brothers)
    "Word kids"
    Summary: Their two-week trip to Hawaii nearly turns to disaster for Chad and Ryan Bartlett as they experience a volcanic eruption, a tidal wave, an earthquake, and a dream-like encounter with an angel.
    ISBN 0–8499–3360–9
    [1. Brothers—Fiction.   2. Hawaii—Fiction.   3. Natural disasters—Fiction.   4. Adventure and adventures—Fiction.   5. Christian life—Fiction.] I. Title. II. Series: Elwood, Roger. Bartlett brothers.
PZ.E554Di 1992
[Fic]—dc20   92–7294
                                       CIP
                                       AC

Printed in the United States of America

2 3 4 5 6 7 8 9 RRD 9 8 7 6 5 4 3 2 1

To
those patient with me at Word
—all my love

 # One

Though it was a dangerous goal for someone of his advanced age, the old man nevertheless wanted to climb Diamond Head before he died. He had lived in one area or another on Oahu all his life, but the the old man had no Hawaiian blood himself.

Because of this, in some respects, native Hawaiians would never really consider him anything but a *haole,* or foreigner. His neighbors through the years had almost always come from Hawaiian families. Their native roots went back a hundred years or, sometimes, quite a bit more.

But while he wasn't accepted nearly as much as he would have liked, he wasn't rejected outright either.

And now he had a chance to make a dream, a crazy, dangerous dream come true.

Diamond Head . . .

The old man had been over the famous volcano countless times by private plane, by helicopter, or by jetliner.

But his *final goal in life* was to climb it—to stand at the rim, to look down inside. And this morning, he had started up the side, which was covered with the rich plant life typical of most of the Hawaiian islands.

Heat.

The old man knew that such heat was unusual this early in the day.

His eyes opened wide!

The heat couldn't have been coming from the early morning sun so much as . . . from Diamond Head itself!

He decided, instantly, that that was impossible. The volcano had been extinct for a very long time.

The old man continued his climb by digging into the side of the familiar landmark, trying to dislodge as little dirt and plant life as possible.

He was halfway up when he began to feel very tired and stopped to rest.

Steam.

He saw it as he looked up at the rim.

Steam drifting over the edge.

What an odor, ugh! he remarked to himself.

He climbed a bit further.

Without warning, there was a scream.

The old man looked straight up, back at the rim.

Someone had fallen, a large body, covered with flames, heading directly toward him.

An instant later, the eruption started . . .

The gentle morning trade winds blew in off the clear, beautiful Pacific Ocean, as Ryan and Chad Bartlett sat on the colorful veranda of the Royal Hawaiian Hotel. This landmark building, with its long porch and bright pink color scheme, was set back from the main bustling shopping district of Waikiki Beach.

They were scheduled to stay in Honolulu for a few days of their two-week trip to Hawaii. With Honolulu as their temporary base, originally the two boys and their father had planned to drive around that island, Oahu, and then make arrangements to fly on to Kauai, Molokai, Maui, and The Big Island.

"First contest we ever won!" Chad exclaimed. "Too bad Dad was delayed by government business in South Africa."

"Well, it wasn't exactly a contest," Ryan replied as he drank from a tall, thin glass of some pink-colored guava juice he had learned to like a lot better than pineapple juice.

"Sure it was, Ryan. We entered. We won. Hey, what's the difference, anyway?"

All of a sudden, Ryan felt like the older brother.

It was an essay co—," he started to say.

"See!" Chad proclaimed victoriously. "You were about to say contest, weren't you?"

"I was not," Ryan insisted.

"What then?"

"*Competition*, that's what."

"Yeah, yeah," Chad remarked teasingly. Then he saw a girl at the far end of the veranda where she also was enjoying the hotel's famous buffet breakfast.

Ryan noticed Chad's new interest and sighed to himself.

Showing through his tank top, his brother's muscular body along with his good looks always equaled girls. When I go around dressed in something like that, all I attract is pity, Ryan thought.

"She's cute," Chad stated the obvious, for if she weren't, he would hardly have been reacting to her the way he was.

"Go meet her. I know you're dying to," Ryan told him, feeling more irritable than he liked to admit. This was especially odd in view of where they were. He loved Hawaii with its bright sun, its beautiful turquoise-blue ocean, and gentle breezes filled with all kinds of exotic scents.

Chad started to stand, then hesitated.

"Ryan?" he said.

"What is it?"

"You're acting strange."

4

"So what's different?"

"Seriously, are you all right?"

Ryan looked across at him.

"As in healthy and happy to be in paradise and all that? Sure, Chad, I guess I'm all right then."

"You're holding back. What is it?"

Ryan shivered a bit.

"You're cold?" Chad asked.

"It's 78 degrees now. How can I be cold?"

"Then why are you shivering?"

Ryan gulped. He loved his brother, but he seldom gave Chad much credit for real sensitivity in a situation like the present one. And now Chad was showing just that!

"Because I feel strange," Ryan admitted.

"Strange? Define strange."

"It's the same way I feel when Dad's in danger. It's hard to explain."

"I can see that. For someone who's usually so good with words, you're suddenly tongue-tied."

Ryan chuckled.

"I deserved that, I guess," he replied.

His gaze drifted toward Diamond Head, seen clearly in the distance.

Smoke!

Ryan sat up straight in his seat.

"Chad!" he said. "Look!"

"Look at what?" his brother asked dumbly.

"Diamond Head. Look at that smoke."

5

Chad now noticed it, too.

"Some brush on fire," he remarked. "It happens."

"I'm sure it does. But this is—."

His words were cut off by the sound of sirens.

Murmuring broke out among the various hotel guests who were also having breakfast on the veranda, a favorite spot for tourists. Right at the beach, it was surrounded by lush tropical semi-jungle. And it was hard to tell whether this had been its original state or if the jungle had been recreated. But the green and scarlet and yellow and pink were beautiful anyway.

Abruptly a short man who looked as though he easily could be of pure Hawaiian blood entered the veranda area, chattering excitedly, *"Wikiwiki, wikiwiki, wikiwiki!"*

Then he stood quietly for a moment, his face red, obviously embarrassed that he had slipped into his native tongue, which none of the visitors present could understand.

"I must ask you to follow me," he said, very, very nervously.

"What's the problem?" a large woman to his left demanded in a loud, hoarse voice.

"Someone from the Honolulu Police Department will explain."

"Police?" her male companion, also very big, asked. "Hey, what gives, mister?"

As though on cue, the ground rumbled beneath them.

"An earthquake?" Chad whispered to his brother.

"No, look!" Ryan replied, pointing toward Diamond Head.

That distant landmark seemed to be going through convulsions, shooting forth huge bursts of molten rock and sending it gushing over the sides of that familiarly-shaped crater, and down onto a—.

Another hotel at the base!

Since it was morning, many hotel guests were still asleep. When they were awakened by a roaring sound, and the massive shaking of the earth beneath them, they thought first of a strong earthquake.

Within a short while, lava had surrounded the main structure, which was ten stories high, and buried smaller ones on the hotel grounds.

Panic took over. In the lobby, people who had planned a day's tour of Oahu were heading frantically toward the nearest exits.

Most were too late. Lava came through the front entrance and through windows. Screaming men, women, and children ran for the stairs in a desperate race from the growing mass of molten rock.

Higher and higher they climbed. Higher and higher the lava rose. The careless ones slipped and fell into its red-hot mass. A handful made it to the top floor and hurried to windows and doorways that gave a view of their surroundings.

Diamond Head looked like a gigantic bathtub, but instead of water overflowing it, there were huge rivers of steamy, orange-red jello-thick molten rock.

Abruptly the building started to sway! Screams tore through the air. The middle of the floor literally became a bubbling pool of lava mixed with wood and concrete and steel.

Everyone ran in terror to the large outside patio. They could hear the sounds of helicopters, three large ones that had left Pearl Harbor minutes before.

Rope ladders were dropped down to the people. One by one, they started to climb up to the hovering copters—one at each end of the patio as well as another in the middle.

The elderly had the worst time of it. But others younger than they helped them, and soldiers pulled them inside each helicopter.

Seconds after the last guest had made it partway up, the entire hotel building collapsed, sending a burst of heat like a bomb blast against those still clinging to the ladders. The blast even rocked the copters, and the pilots struggled to keep from losing control.

Those who could bear to look saw below them a $50-million building disappear as though it were nothing more than a pasteboard movie set.

Buildings had sprung up over the years in nearly every direction around Diamond Head. This was prime real estate. Most were expensive residences, a large percentage costing well over a million dollars each.

All were destroyed. Families had little time to evacuate. They could not grab even any valuables. They lost everything they had.

Much later, in the mopping up aftermath of the eruption, great numbers of bewildered men, women, and children could be seen stumbling around, disbelieving, in the smoking wreckage.

Dozens who didn't make it were covered by the lava. But dozens more managed to find their way into the interior of Oahu, to settlements that had been erected by the original missionaries two hundred years earlier, and which were still maintained.

Among them were Ryan and Chad Bartlett and a little boy named Benny they had found as they were leaving the center of Honolulu and heading inland.

 **Two**

The three of them were huddled in an open field surrounded by jungle growth. Exotic plants were so densely packed together that hiking was almost impossible. This was a secluded part of Hawaii that had remained basically "pure" despite long years of wildly increasing building activity elsewhere on the island. In other areas residences and office structures now stood on land once covered with vegetation like this.

Ryan, Chad, and little Benny were not alone.

They had been joined by a dozen or more survivors, some of whom had found the spot inland by pure chance, others who were aware of it from either living on Oahu or as the result of previous visits to the island.

Ryan and Chad long had known about the old missionary camp. They had visited it before and knew how to get there. But it was quite some distance. At one point in their flight from Honolulu, neither of them knew if they would ever make it so far.

They had to get through the enormous crowds of people in cars or on motorcycles or, like themselves, being forced to run for it on foot.

At one point soon after they left the hotel, Ryan and Chad rescued a little boy even younger than Benny. The child would have been crushed to death if Chad hadn't grabbed him in time. The boy's parents failed to notice the crumbling storefront to their right.

"How can we ever thank you?" the young mother and father asked Chad.

They all agreed to keep in touch, if they survived this terrible disaster. Soon the parents and the little boy became separated from Ryan and Chad. They were caught up in a crowd going a different direction. Chad yelled after them, but they couldn't hear him because of the noise of falling buildings and the hysterical mob. Gripped by raging panic, many people were thinking far less clearly than they should have been.

Fortunately, after many trips to the Hawaiian Islands over the past few years, Ryan and Chad knew their way around Oahu. Others, however, in that huge mass of screaming and running and pushing bodies didn't have that advantage.

In fact, like the little boy and his mother and father, others were headed in the wrong direction, running blindly toward areas down-slope from Diamond Head, which was exactly the direction the lava was flowing. But people thinking more clearly, like Ryan and Chad, were going inland toward the mountainous sections of Oahu!

"Listen!" a middle-aged man next to them shouted as he caught some news on his transistor radio.

"The eruption of once-dormant—not extinct, as many supposed—Diamond Head in the state of Hawaii has been joined by other catastrophic occurrences elsewhere in the world. There has been a major earthquake just outside Tokyo, Japan. Hundreds of millions of dollars in damage. The worst flood in more than a century has ravaged villages and towns all along the western coast of India.

"And within the continental United States, in the midst of farmlands all through the Midwest, locusts have returned in large numbers after an absence of many years.

"What we are seeing all over the world is like a scene from a biblical story of prophecy coming to pass right before our eyes!"

Ryan and Chad glanced at one another.

"Biblical prophecy," Ryan whispered. "Over public radio!"

"Yeah," his brother remarked. "I hate to say this, but I don't think it will do anything but add

13

to the panic. And what about those who are converted now? How sincere will they be a year from now?"

"You're talking about foxhole Christianity," said Ryan.

"Exactly. People who turn to God only in time of trouble."

"But sometimes disaster can change a person forever. I guess we can only hope these people keep their faith when times are good," said Ryan.

Chad and Ryan had seen plenty of people praying during the mad dash they had made out Highway T, which was the main thoroughfare that cut directly down the center of Oahu.

Some of these people were knocked over and trampled on by other men and women who were thinking only of escape . . . escape from the lava that had reached the outskirts of Honolulu . . . escape from the toxic fumes in the air . . . escape from the spreading panic of which they all were a real part.

Other people were in prayer along the side of the highway itself.

That was where they had found Benny, kneeling beside a car that was a battered pile of twisted metal. They came up to him slowly. When the little boy realized that Ryan and Chad were next to him, he looked up, his expression brightening.

"I was asking God for help," he said, a little smile crossing his face. "Mom and Dad told me He listens real good."

At first Ryan and Chad assumed that the two bodies in the wrecked car must have been those of his parents.

Wrong.

As it turned out, Benny had become separated from his mother and father. And a young couple had hurriedly taken him into their car as they rushed for safety. Benny said they were going to help him find his parents.

 # Three

"**A**re we doomed?" the man with the radio asked. The expression on his face was full of fear as he turned to them.

"I don't know any more than you do, mister," Chad replied. "Nobody does except God Himself."

"But you were saying something about the Bible. I mean, I never paid much attention over the years. What does it say?"

"Pretty complicated to deal with in a few minutes," Ryan put in.

"Please try," the man asked urgently. "I'm interested. Maybe there are more like me here."

A murmur of assent.

Everyone else in that isolated spot had suddenly turned toward Ryan and Chad.

Ryan stood, feeling very uncomfortable being at the center of everybody's attention and wishing they had their father with them.

But they didn't.

Andrew Bartlett was in South Africa for meetings between the leaders of the warring tribes as well as the government and the two main black rebel groups. The meetings had run a few days longer than planned or he would have been with his sons in Hawaii.

Ryan felt that he and Chad were more alone now, in the middle of Hawaii, than just about any other time or place in their lives.

That included the time when Ryan accidently discovered a terrorist plot to blow up a nuclear power plant. Even then Andrew Bartlett managed to make it back to them, all the way from the Middle East.

And there was the huge and elegant *S. S. Oceanic*, a cruise ship that sank in shark-infested Caribbean waters, nearly taking the three of them with it. But at least they were all three together through that terrifying experience.

After nearly drowning, Andrew Bartlett was rescued, along with his sons, and finally another living nightmare ended, one that had started out as a relaxing vacation away from just the sort of thing that had happened anyway!

It was the same during their run-in with killers associated with the Forbidden River drug cartel. Even in the midst of supposedly safe-and-secure Washington, D.C., their activities proved dangerous, just as Andrew Bartlett was starting his job as National Security Advisor.

And other times—Andrew Bartlett was always around or able to get to them before it was too late.

But, now, by the time he found out what had happened with Diamond Head, it could take a day or more to reach them.

For one thing, it might not be easy for anyone, including Andrew Bartlett, to get a plane on a moment's notice. Even those in high-level governmental circles had their limitations. And under no circumstances could any traveling time be cut from a flight beginning at the very bottom tip of Africa and extending all the way on to the Hawaiian Islands thousands of miles away. After all, airplanes could go just so fast.

We might be long dead by the time Dad arrives, Ryan told himself. *Even though we're now safe, no one here has any way of telling what might happen to us next.*

"Aren't you gonna tell us anything, kid?" a coarse voice broke into his thoughts.

He looked at the more than a dozen men and women, most of them tourists wearing bold-print, native-looking clothes.

All seemed desperate as they gathered in front of Ryan.

"Wait a minute!" a very overweight man grumbled out loud. "Why, he's just a scrawny, little wimp."

Wimp? He calls me a wimp, Ryan said to himself. *Better that than a sweaty overstuffed—!*

He had really become good at controlling his emotions. In fact, he didn't even lash back at the man. His temper was not as bad as it would have been a year ago in such a situation.

That energized Ryan. He uttered a quick, silent prayer for the Lord's guidance, then told his listeners what he had been able to learn about the part of biblical prophecy that dealt with upheaval on Planet Earth just prior to the Second Coming of Christ.

They all could see a great deal from the elevated location of the camp. With nearly a 360-degree view, they could see all the way from the Kailua coast down to the breathtaking turn at Sea Life Park, on through to Waikiki Beach.

At another time, it would have been quite an experience but now all they could see was chaos. Even as they watched, the eastern side of Diamond Head caved in completely, and the lava flow increased.

As night came, the sight was dazzling. Blood-red portions of liquid rock and soil mixed with those that were bright orange in color.

"Praise God that Cindy isn't here. I'm glad she's visiting on the mainland," Ryan whispered, not wanting to awaken any of those who had managed to fall asleep, especially little Benny.

Cindy was a friend who worked at Sea Life Park.

"You're right," Chad agreed. "Wonder what's happened to the dolphins and the seals at the park?"

Nearby a woman in her thirties overheard them and said, "Sorry for interrupting, but I . . . I passed by that area."

"What about the animals?"

"It was something!" she said. "I could see three dolphins actually helping people!"

"Helping?" Ryan asked.

"Yes, part of the wall that separated them from the ocean collapsed. They started to swim out to sea. But then the three of them stopped suddenly when they saw several people with their clothes afire. Those dolphins swam back and . . . and—"

The woman was nearly overcome with emotion.

Chad inched over to her and put his arm around her.

"That's okay," he said. "You don't have to tell us all the details, you really don't."

"I do!" she exclaimed. "It was so beautiful. It really was. They started splashing, splashing, splashing at the water with their tails. They seemed to know that this might do the trick!"

She looked up at Chad, her cheeks wet.

"They put out the fires," she said. "I think they saved the lives of those people!"

"That's wonderful, really wonderful," Ryan said softly, earnestly. "But, to be honest, it doesn't surprise me, ma'am. I know firsthand that dolphins can do incredible things."

And he proceeded to recount his experiences just after being knocked off the *S. S. Oceanic.*

Others heard them talking and came over, gathering around. It was well after midnight when they finally ran out of stories about dogs, cats, monkeys, dolphins, and other animals intervening in the lives of human beings to help them survive.

**Four**

Morning came every bit as beautifully as it always did in the Hawaiian Islands. Despite various volcanic eruptions, tropical storms, earthquakes or whatever else, the sun rose each morning, the vegetation was as multi-colored as usual, and nothing else changed. It was a pattern set countless centuries before.

During the night they had watched fires below. Now with daylight they could see the smoke from these. Some quite large, others barely visible. The air continued to be filled with the odors of burning things and the distinctive smell of hot lava itself.

"Every island, every continent began this way," a short, bald, scholarly looking man was musing out loud. "The process of birth is also the process of destruction, as we're seeing now."

The man was standing next to Ryan and Chad.

"My name is Ryan Bartlett," Ryan introduced himself.

"Elmer Kane," came the reply, along with an extended hand.

"And I'm Chad Bartlett," Chad told him cheerfully, as he, too, shook the man's hand. "How are you, sir?"

"As good as can be expected . . . I mean, that is . . . for a man fleeing a lava flow like someone in a scene from *One Million B. C.*!"

Chad laughed.

"Life imitating movies," he said.

"There are some movies *my* life won't imitate," Kane replied.

"I agree," Chad told him.

Little Benny was becoming squirmy.

"Cute kid," Kane observed. "Is he your brother?"

"No," Ryan replied. "Benny here became separated from his parents. We're taking care of him."

"You know what bugs me about this?" Kane commented, a heavy frown on his broad forehead.

"About the eruption?" Ryan asked.

"Yes, exactly that. Certain people knew there was activity going on weeks ago."

Ryan's mouth dropped open.

"You're serious?"

"Very serious, son. But somebody very high up in the tourism commission managed to keep the contents of that report secret. The seismologist who recorded the changes in earth movement activity was threatened."

"With what?" Chad put in.

"With being fired and, also, with something more violent because simply losing his job was a threat that just didn't work."

What Kane had been saying was overheard by just about everyone else in the group.

Several raised their voices, angry that their lives had been jeopardized because of the dishonest and dangerous motives of at least one individual who was more interested in profit than safety.

Both Ryan and Chad were thinking about their father. This was the kind of thing he should know about. Maybe he could even find a way to help them. If only there was a way to reach him.

"Does anyone have a shortwave radio?" Ryan asked hopefully. But he realized the chances of that were slim, since they were in such an isolated location.

No one responded with a yes.

Benny tugged at Ryan's hand. The boy was pointing toward one of the old huts that dotted the clearing.

"What is it?" he asked.

"R-r-r-a-a-d-i-o," he said, with a stutter.

At first Ryan couldn't understand him.

Then someone from the group spoke up.

"It's easy to see you got no small kids," the woman said. "He's saying 'radio!' I saw him wandering near that hut when he had to, well, you know—."

Ryan ran to the hut and looked in. There inside was a shortwave radio. Benny must have heard a voice coming from the box earlier that morning. But to him it was just a radio.

Thank you, Lord, Ryan prayed silently. *Now, I ask You to help me remember how to use it.*

Ryan went inside, Chad behind him, and everyone else following them.

"Hey, wait, we can't just blurt out Dad's secret code," Chad whispered into his brother's ear.

"What choice do we have?" Ryan replied. "Dad's got to know what's been going on here. After all, we may not make it off this island alive."

"I realize that, but we've got to be careful."

Ryan smiled as an idea hit him.

"We'll just contact the White House switchboard and ask for Dad's office," he said. "We don't need that secret stuff!"

"You'll never make it," Chad told him. "They won't believe you. The operator gets thousands of crazy calls."

"Watch me," Ryan said confidently.

In less than two minutes, he had managed to talk his way through to his father's office! Ryan's message would be forwarded to South Africa.

Everyone who had gathered around that little hut began to applaud and cheer.

Andrew Bartlett was furious. After he got Ryan's message, he could barely control himself.

Tourist dollars placed above the welfare of tens of thousands of people! His mind screamed in real anger.

Mr. Bartlett sat at a temporary desk in the tiny South African office reserved for him during his visit to that country, as National Security Advisor to the President of the United States.

He found that his whole body was trembling.

My sons could die! All because of what amounts to blood money in some greedy official's bank account! But what about everybody else? Oahu is the hub of the Hawaiian Islands. All air traffic goes through there. The potential for destruction is beyond calculation!

He called Washington, D.C., on a special emergency phone line. After less than a minute, Mr. Bartlett was connected directly with the Secretary of Defense.

"Hello, Andy, what seems to be the trouble, friend?" the Secretary asked as soon as he came on the line.

"Diamond Head," Mr. Bartlett replied, realizing that the general news would have been well known to such a high United States government official.

"Yes, yes, I know."

"My boys, sir!"

"Ryan and Chad? You mean they're—?"

"Exactly right. I need to get to the islands as soon as possible. What red tape can be eliminated?"

"In your case, a great deal. I'll have a group of fliers join with the Navy guys from Pearl Harbor. We'll send them over from Edwards Air Force Base in California."

"Is there nothing else?" Mr. Bartlett asked, running the risk of seeming to be ungrateful.

"Any ideas?" the Secretary remarked, not taking offense.

"The Concorde? Can we get it?"

"For you?"

"Yes . . . for me. It's the closest and fastest passenger plane I can think of."

There was a pause. Then: "I'll call Paris. Let's see what we can do. It'll mean—."

The Secretary cut himself off, rummaging around in his mind for an alternative that would work.

"What is it, sir?" Mr. Bartlett asked nervously, wondering if some unforeseen hurdle had become apparent.

"Better idea," the Secretary continued, his

thoughts racing. "I'll get the South Africans to fly you part of the way in one of those supersonic models they bought from us a few years ago."

"Not enough range, sir."

"That's true, of course. But I was about to say that, at least, it will get you as far as our base at Guam. Then from there you can go on to Oahu in another plane, which I'll make sure is fueled up and waiting for you without delay. You'll cut air time to half or less."

Mr. Bartlett breathed a sigh of relief.

"Sir?"

"Yes?"

"Praise God for your help."

"And for His own, Andy."

"Thank you, sir, for everything."

"God be with you, Andrew Bartlett."

And with my sons, their father whispered to himself.

# Five

Helicopters.

A dozen or more of these could be seen in the distance, directly over Honolulu. And along the coast there were ships from Pearl Harbor and elsewhere.

Chad stood with his brother and the others, watching the distant action from a lookout point near the old missionary camp. "Pearl Harbor probably got through this with less damage than anywhere else on the south side of Oahu. It's farther away from Diamond Head than Honolulu. And, all that water in the harbor would be a natural shield."

To their left the little group could see the jagged outline of the volcano. Its fiery eruptions seemed to have stopped for the moment. But there were no guarantees that there would not be more. Now a kind of black, steamy, sooty mist hung over that southeastern section of Oahu.

It was obvious no one knew what to do, no leader as such had yet been appointed.

"Ryan," Chad whispered into his brother's ear. "It could be a problem, you know, just staying here."

"You want to go back down there?" Ryan asked.

"Hey, think, will you? No one really knows we're here. We told Dad what was happening but—."

Ryan had to admit that Chad was right.

He was so excited about making contact with their father's office and getting word to him about what had happened in general, that he had forgotten to pinpoint their location. He had failed to tell him they were in the geographic middle of Oahu, on an elevated portion of land that had been hewn out of the surrounding jungle.

Ryan had an idea.

"Chad, I think we should head in the opposite direction, to the Kaneohe Bay area. The lava couldn't have reached all that distance, or we would have seen some evidence of it from where we are now.

"There are small communities along the coast. Help will come to them a lot faster because, after all, the authorities know that they're there. And residents will have radios, food, whatever we need to keep us going."

"Great idea," Chad admitted. "Why don't we tell everybody what we've got in mind."

Ryan turned and faced the others.

"I don't think we should go on staying here," he said, raising his voice so that all of the others could hear him. "Unless someone spots us from a helicopter or an airplane, we could be here a lot longer than necessary."

"Where do you propose that all of us head, son?" an elderly man asked. His tone was one of growing respect, all the more amazing in view of how Ryan looked every bit the part of a typically uncertain fourteen-year-old boy. With his five-foot-three height and scrawny build, he was the exact opposite of his muscular brother in appearance, and hardly the type to give advice to adults.

"I doubt that there's very much destruction on the windward side, at least not any caused by what has happened at Diamond Head. Besides, it will be easier to connect with help whenever it comes if we're in what is a known area of population."

The group broke out into spontaneous applause.

Ryan's face flushed as red as the brightly colored shirt he was wearing.

Andrew Bartlett was halfway to the U. S. air base on the Pacific island of Guam when a message came over the jet's shortwave radio.

"Earthquakes throughout Japan have ceased, but aftershocks remain an ever-present danger. There is also concern about the chances of tidal waves from Australia across the Pacific, all the way east to Hawaii as well as North and South America. This has caused a growing sense of panic and—."

Mr. Bartlett blocked the rest out of his mind, concentrating only on part of what he had heard and repeating it over and over to himself.

The chances of tidal waves from Australia across the Pacific, all the way east to Hawaii. . . .

"Lord Jesus," he prayed out loud, "please stay with Ryan and Chad. Please guide them through this."

After Mr. Bartlett had finished praying, he noticed the pilot glancing at him.

"You're a Christian?" the man asked, the answer obvious.

"Yes, I am," he replied.

"Guess that comes in handy in your business."

"What do you mean?"

"Well, isn't it kind of like having your own personal good luck charm, sir?"

Mr. Bartlett struggled to keep from losing his temper.

"We pray, my family and I, in good times and bad. We aren't foxhole Christians. We thank the Lord for whatever comes our way!"

34

"Are you serious? I mean, if your sons didn't make it, you would still praise God and all that?"

"Not easily, no. It would be very difficult, but in the end I would. Yes, I would. Because I wouldn't consider them gone for good. We would just be separated for a while, for we'll be together again in heaven."

"Then, if you don't mind me asking, why are you praying for their survival here, now, in the flesh?"

Mr. Bartlett hesitated for a moment, realizing that the pilot had made a valid point by saying what he did.

"While we are here in this life, we love, we laugh, we cry, we do the normal things any other human being does," he finally replied. "And part of the human experience is sorrow and pain over the loss of those we love very, very much. Someday that will no longer be the case, but right at this very moment it is.

"I can't live as though we're already in heaven. I have to face what every man, every father must —the possibility of losing his children, however awful that might be."

The pilot turned his head away and pretended to be studying the jet's gauges. Mr. Bartlett could sense that his words were having an effect.

"As a husband, I've faced the tragic death of my sons' mother," he continued. "Being a

Christian helped, but it didn't conquer my depression. Because of that loss, I fear all the more for my sons. They're all I have left. They're all that physically remains of the relationship between my wife and myself."

For an instant the pilot bowed his head.

"Are you all right?" Mr. Bartlett inquired.

"Yes . . . " the man said after a moment or so. "I have no one left, no one at all. My family died in a riot near Capetown."

"Caused by the black opposition groups?"

"No, they were accidentally killed by government riot police. I don't blame the men responsible. It was a form of warfare in those days, and in war the innocent suffer. But I do miss my wife, my son, and my daughter. They didn't die on the spot, but hours later in a nearby hospital."

"Were they believers?" Mr. Bartlett asked.

"Yes, but I myself wasn't then, nor can I honestly say that I am now. If only I could know the comfort, the peace of having the same conviction of where they are that you have about your wife."

"It's possible that you can, you know."

"That's pretty easy to say. But how? I've done so many wrong things, sir. You couldn't imagine some of what I've gotten into, you really couldn't."

Mr. Bartlett reached out and touched his shoulder.

"It can happen now, my friend, right where we are," he said knowingly, "in the cramped quarters of this jet."

By the time they touched down at the Guam base, the pilot had chosen a fresh life as a Christian. And Andrew Bartlett knew his new friend would never be the same again.

 # Six

Climbing down from that mountain plateau proved to be no problem for most of the men and women in the little group. And it was actually easy for a teenager as muscular and athletic as Chad. But for the elderly and Ryan, that was another story entirely.

One woman in her late seventies cut a gash in her left leg. Her husband who was five years older nearly dislocated his shoulder and had to wear a makeshift sling. Ryan's legs, bare because of his shorts, were badly bruised.

Finally they were standing next to a major highway that led in the direction they wanted to go.

Everywhere they looked the turmoil caused by the eruption was evident: Cars had smashed into one another, bits and pieces of clothing were strewn about, asphalt was cracked in a number of spots.

Considering, though, all the confusion and panic on the southern side of Oahu, the northern side seemed far less affected. It was much more thinly populated. Urban growth had been restricted for a number of years after outcries by environmentalists that the developers were robbing the island of the special look and feel, the atmosphere, that had made it so attractive for so long.

Ahead and to their left, the beach to their right, were some houses, built on the side of a mountain.

Unlike Maui and Molokai and the others, Oahu had considerably less flatlands. That was why building activity tended to be concentrated in and around Honolulu. Back in the vicinity of the old missionary settlement, there was quite a bit of flatter jungle territory, but this had been declared off-limits for ecological and historical reasons.

"That smell," Ryan said, wrinkling up his nose at its continuing unpleasantness. "I wonder if it'll ever end."

"You'll remember it for a long time," Chad told him. "I guess that'll be the case for all of us."

The family in the first house they approached was instantly friendly and helpful. But the building itself was quite small.

"My cousin lives there!" the Hawaiian husband

and wife said all at once. "They will be glad to help."

In a matter of minutes, fifteen strangers were taken into three different homes, and given hospitality beyond anything they could have guessed a short while earlier.

Ryan, Chad, Benny, and a Mr. and Mrs. Saussman went to the first home.

Soon Benny was busy playing with the two children who lived there.

"I come from New York City," Abe Saussman commented as he sat beside Ryan and Chad in the living room. "You can't begin to imagine how this group would have been treated at some places there."

"How's that?" Chad asked.

"Doors slammed in our faces, that's what!" he proclaimed, as his wife, Winnie, murmured agreement.

"I think there's a reason," Ryan said.

"Yeah, what's that?" Abe Saussman asked coarsely, but with a hint of deep respect for this fourteen-year-old.

"New Yorkers don't face calamity as much as, say, Californians do," Ryan went on. "Sure, you have crime, yet crime forces people to protect themselves and not worry about the other guy."

"But in California there are earthquakes," Saussman said, catching on to Ryan's point. "Wondering about The Big One, yeah, that's it. They never know when it's gonna happen. And they may need each other to survive."

Saussman, a tough-looking man, seemed proud of himself . . . like a little boy who had discovered a special truth and wanted to tell everyone about it.

"You got it on the money," Ryan said encouragingly. "But, to be honest, there is something else."

Saussman rubbed his broad chin.

"Smog?" he offered.

"True, but that's like crime. It's always there. I was thinking, sir, of fires."

With that, Saussman fell silent. Chad was quick to notice the change.

"Anything wrong, sir?" Chad asked, concerned that the man might be ill, or hurting.

After a moment the man spoke up again.

"I don't like fires. I lost my mother and father in one. The fires we've been seeing in Honolulu brought back some bad memories."

"Sorry . . . " Ryan said.

"No problem, kid. In this life we all have these nightmares that we have to deal with."

Ryan and Chad both knew that was true. They had their own nightmares: The family car blackened, twisted . . . their mother's lifeless body thrown from it by the force of the blast.

"Yes, sir," Chad told him. "My brother and I know what you mean."

 **Seven**

Hours passed. The telephones weren't working on the north side of the island. But at least the homes there still had electricity and were receiving news by radio and television. As Chad and Ryan and the others in that first home gathered around the TV, the news was both encouraging and distressing.

The eruptions had ceased altogether, though the shape of Diamond Head itself had been permanently changed, no longer a safe, attractive landmark.

Scores of people had died. The miracle was that there hadn't been hundreds, or even thousands of deaths. But something else entered the picture.

"No longer will the state of Hawaii be the same," the male TV commentator said as he stood amidst the wreckage. "No longer will life be lived in a carefree and leisurely manner. Gone will be the assumption that Diamond Head, one of the best-known landmarks in the entire United States, is simply something to look at, something on pretty postcards or travel posters. Diamond Head will be viewed as nothing more than a menace, to be feared from this moment forward.

"How can life go on as before? How can buildings be erected, homes built, plans made for the future? Any day, any moment, Diamond Head could spout forth its fury and once again disrupt the peaceful life we know here on Oahu."

Everybody watching gasped with amazement.

"That's putting everything on the line," Saussman remarked. "I wonder how long that guy will hold his job after this?"

"He was just telling the truth," Chad observed. "But in an economy that is, to a great extent, based upon tourism, truth like that can mean disaster."

It was late in the day. Everyone was getting restless. They were tired of just sitting around, watching television, and waiting for help.

Ryan heard a sound.

"Turn off the TV!" he shouted.

When Saussman did just that, the rest of them heard what Ryan had caught a moment before.

The sound of a helicopter overheard.

They all rushed out to the front porch, which was made of grey-black hewn lava rock and extended across the full length of that house. Those in the other two houses had done the same.

Three large helicopters. All landed on the beach across the highway from the houses.

The local families and their guests waited for the sandstorm created by the whirling helicopter blades to stop. Then they all rushed across the highway to stand on the beach in front of the helicopters.

A growing number of other people from various houses along the beach began to join them.

A lieutenant from Pearl Harbor on the other side of the island approached the swelling crowd.

"My name is Lieutenant Aaron Muncie," he told them.

He looked a lot like Chad probably would in fifteen or twenty years—tall and handsome with a broad, muscular frame. He spoke with the confidence of a man who could handle any situation, whatever the urgency.

"Everything is under control on the other side of the island," he said reassuringly. "Shelters are being set up in several locations. And we have the privilege of special assistance from someone in the White House. That's right! I'd like to introduce the President's national security advisor, who has made the trip for quite personal reasons."

Just behind him, Andrew Bartlett poked his head out and jumped down on the sand.

"Dad!" Ryan and Chad shouted all at once.

They ran to him, and he to them. Then as the three embraced, a cheer arose from the gathered crowd, but it was cut short.

"Look!" someone said.

All eyes turned toward the surf, which was withdrawing from the shore, as though being sucked away!

"What in the world is causing that?" Saussman said loudly.

The lieutenant leaned over and hurriedly whispered something in Andrew Bartlett's ear.

"Chad, Ryan," their father said in the lowest voice possible. "Get on the copter as quickly but as calmly as you can."

Without delay or protest they took Benny with them and boarded the helicopter. After making sure Benny was safetly seated in the rear, the boys joined their father at the door to help others climb on board.

By that time, everyone had been instructed to board the helicopters.

"But my home!" one woman protested. "The danger is over. What's going on now?"

The answer was apparent in a matter of seconds.

The surf was no longer withdrawing. It had gathered together into a thirty-foot-high wall of water—and though no one there realized it, there were other massive walls like that one all around Oahu at that very second.

"Tidal wave!" someone shouted.

In seconds the helicopters took off. The one carrying the Bartletts, Benny, and a few others was the last to leave the shore. The tidal wave hit before it could fly out of reach. The pilot and Lieutenant Muncie were knocked out of it. But the three Bartletts, who were also still near the door, managed to hold on as the copter was smashed against a hard stone jetty, crumbling into a hopelessly jagged pile of twisted metal. When the second huge wave hit, moments later, the helicopter was torn loose and taken out to sea.

 **Eight**

Incredibly, Ryan, Chad, and Andrew Bartlett were all crammed together into a single air pocket. As the helicopter was being tossed about by ocean currents, they had been temporarily sealed off from the invading water, both doors jammed shut.

Not for long—either the ocean would eventually find its way into the compartment, or they would suffocate.

All three were cut and bruised, their nerves frazzled, but none seemed to be seriously hurt. They hoped that Benny, too, was safe somewhere farther back in the helicopter where he had been sitting with others.

"What do we do?" Ryan said, panicky.

"We pray, but we can't expect God necessarily to reach down and open a door for us," Andrew Bartlett told them honestly. "I don't know what we do, son. This is worse than the situation aboard the *S. S. Oceanic*.

"We can't just keep on talking, unfortunately," Mr. Bartlett reminded them. "That'll eat up the oxygen more quickly."

They all fell into silence.

A short while later, something happened that they could never have expected.

The helicopter was being moved!

"What in the—?" Chad started to say.

"Currents must be stronger," Mr. Bartlett said. "That means another tidal wave!"

They braced for the sudden, violent wrenching motion that would indicate his guess was right on the mark.

It didn't happen. But the copter kept on moving.

Ryan was about to speak when his father brought a finger to his lips, reminding him not to talk. The question of the oxygen being wasted was far more important than anything any of them might want to say.

The movement continued, not at all roughly, either. They could see through the shatterproof glass of the copter's front window. The ocean floor seemed to be amazingly calm. There was no indication of the awful turbulence that would have been part of another thirty-foot-high wave.

A reef shark passed by. To the right they could see a large squid. There were schools of rainbow-colored fish.

So calm down here, Ryan thought. *It's a whole different world, insulated from any of the catastrophe above sea level. So calm, beautiful, serene!*

Suddenly a thirteen-foot great white shark appeared, heading straight for them.

Lord, is this it? Andrew Bartlett prayed silently. *If so, please, let it be without a lot of pain for my sons and me, just before we enter Your Kingdom. Thank You, Lord, in the name of Jesus, Your Son, our Savior.*

Instantly, perhaps the most extraordinary sight any of them had ever seen took place right before their eyes. Several dozen dolphins headed toward the huge shark. A whole school of them!

The helicopter started to sink to the ocean floor. There wasn't so much as a thud as it landed. The three passengers inside could see the dolphins hammering away at the shark, butting it with their tough snouts.

Several of the dolphins were lost to the deadly teeth in the shark's monstrous mouth, but, after just a short while, even the great white could not withstand the constant battering. It swam off, unsteadily, then stopped suddenly, blood spurting from its mouth, and turned over on its side, dead!

"Dad, Dad, those dolphins were what was floating us along!" Ryan stuttered, overwhelmed.

"We'll discuss it later!" Mr. Bartlett reminded his son. "No air, no breathe, no live! Is that clear?"

Ryan nodded and was silent, watching with his father and his brother as several members of the school of dolphins came back and gathered around the helicopter.

Some of them nudged their way underneath the wreckage and began to balance it on top of their backs. The others moved along on either side as a kind of "armed" escort.

The rest of the school must have been hovering out of sight a little distance away the first time, Ryan thought. *Now they're taking no chances at all.*

None of the three of them could tell how long it actually took for the dolphins to transport the copter to where they wanted it.

Suddenly—

"Dad, look!" Ryan said, raising his voice. "The ocean floor's sloping upward. We're heading toward shore."

Then something happened.

The copter was slammed off the backs of the dolphins and started to act like a cork in a whirlpool bath!

Another tidal wave!

It was apparent that the dolphins were no match for the turbulence and had to back off, or else they, too, would be destroyed. But this time that very same tremendous pressure sucked the helicopter doors right out of their frames, and the ocean came rushing into the open compartment!

# Nine

Andrew Bartlett thought again and again about what happened next. He thought about it during the months and the years that followed. And he prayed often, each prayer one of earnest thanks for sudden rescue out of a desperate situation . . . for himself and his two sons.

He thought he felt something pulling him, something like a strong hand, firm around his own. Without quite knowing what he was doing, he grabbed what it was, his free hand floundering until it, too, was being held.

Yes, he was being pulled upward, through the vicious currents, through the massive power of the tidal wave . . . upward, as his lungs threatened to collapse, his body desperate for oxygen . . . upward, as though he had merely fallen toward the bottom of a swimming pool and someone with very long arms had caught him and was bringing him back up, out of the water.

Suddenly he blacked out, the rush of pure, blessed, life-giving air too rich just then for his system.

Andrew Bartlett regained consciousness on a black-sand beach nestled in a little cove.

Ryan! Chad! his mind shouted immediately, instinctively. *Oh, Lord, Lord, please don't let them be gone. Don't let them be swept out to sea and lost.* The thought of never seeing them again, never having another chance to tell them how much he loved them was almost more than he could bear.

Then he heard sounds, groaning sounds. They were coming from his left. He turned on his side and looked in that direction.

Chad!

Mr. Bartlett got slowly to his feet and stumbled over to his son. Chad looked up at him.

"You made it, too!" he said as he got unsteadily to his feet.

They embraced one another.

Finally that moment of surging emotion passed. Then both turned and frantically looked around. The blood drained from their faces, and their muscles tightened. Both shouted the same name at the same time.

"Ryan!"

Chad and Mr. Bartlett found Ryan, semi-conscious, on some rocks at one corner of the cove.

He was bruised and bleeding from several cuts, but there were no gashes, as such, and no bones seemed to be broken.

After they got Ryan to the beach, severe exhaustion made all three plop on the sand, unable to move any further.

"I was praying so hard," Chad sobbed. "I was begging the Lord to get the three of us through this nightmare. I . . . I couldn't stand to be spared . . . and lose the two of you. I couldn't. Then while I was in the water the oddest thing happened . . . "

"A hand, Chad," Ryan said weakly. "Did it feel like a strong hand was pulling you out of the water?"

"Exactly!" said his brother, surprised and still barely able to comprehend what had happened.

"Wait a moment, you two," their father said. "Don't assume what you're assuming. We can't be sure. God isn't Someone who gives us miracles on demand, you know."

"But it seemed so real, Dad," Chad protested.

"I know," Mr. Bartlett replied. "I'm just saying that we shouldn't jump to conclusions about this."

Chad and Ryan saw their father's expression.

"Dad, did you experience the same thing?" Chad asked knowingly.

"I did," Mr. Bartlett admitted reluctantly. "It felt just like a hand was pulling me up."

Ryan interrupted.

"That's what happened with me," he told them. "Strong grip but gentle at the same time."

"It could have been our imaginations," Mr. Bartlett remarked. "It could have been nothing more than some strong currents pushing us toward shore."

"Is that what you really think, Dad?"

"No, Ryan, it isn't. None of us can be sure what did happen. We were hardly in a position to be objective about anything."

"Dad?"

"Yes, Chad?"

"I love you."

Ryan spoke the same words.

"Lord," Mr. Bartlett prayed out loud, "Thank You! We're here, alive, and together. What more could we ask just now?"

. . . What more could we ask just now?

They got more, and soon, much more indeed.

Together.

That thought hit them all at pretty much the same time. Often when things got out of hand, and there was danger, Ryan and Chad had to face it alone because their father was usually in a foreign country. Until recently Andrew Bartlett had worked undercover as a secret agent and was almost always in a dangerous situation of his own.

Being trapped on the *S. S. Oceanic,* a doomed Caribbean cruise ship, proved to be an exception—that was an adventure the three of them definitely shared. But when they had a startling confrontation with a longtime Mafioso godfather, Ryan and Chad had to face the consequences alone.

Other such encounters came to mind, two resourceful teenagers forced to deal with adult-sized nightmares!

But, now, after facing volcanic eruptions as well as two tidal waves, they were back together. In the midst of anything else that came their way, the three of them would have each other to help.

"Where do we go?" Ryan asked.

"I'm not sure but there's one thing we won't have to worry about," Mr. Bartlett said, "unlike so many other places."

"No snakes!" Ryan interjected proudly.

"That's exactly right," his father replied. "The mongooses got rid of those a long time ago."

The cove was surrounded by part of a mountain. But it was too steep to climb, especially since all three of them had been weakened by what they had just endured.

"I don't know if I can make it," Mr. Bartlett admitted.

Even Chad, the star athlete, didn't think they could climb up the jagged side.

"Can we just stay here?" Ryan asked. "It's a secluded spot. How can we be sure that anyone will discover us before it's too late?"

"There's a better chance of that than any of us making a climb that we can't handle right now," Chad told him.

Ryan nodded with great reluctance. The truth was that he hated feeling that he had no options, none whatsoever.

"With my computer at home, I'm in charge," he remarked. "I turn it on. I turn it off. I decide what programming I'll use. And how I'll use it. This . . . this not being able to do anything is real frustrating!"

"Son," Mr. Bartlett said, "I suspect that it's the sort of position which the Lord allows from time to time, perhaps to show us that only He is in charge."

Ryan blushed as soon as he heard those words. He knew his father was right. There were few times when the man wasn't.

"So do we just sit here and wait?" he asked, not totally letting go of his annoyance over their situation.

"I suspect we don't have much—," he started to say.

"Dad!" Chad's terrified scream cut him off.

The surf was draining out again, more rapidly than before. They could see the water gather together, and rise up, like some mythological sea monster.

They ran frantically toward what they thought was a solid wall of rock and packed soil. There was no other direction in which to turn.

In less than a minute, this latest tidal wave could easily smash them against the mountainside, and there was no guarantee that they'd survive this time!

 **Ten**

A cave, Dad!" Ryan shouted, pointing to a spot behind some hanging tropical plants.

"I see it, Ryan," Mr. Bartlett said. "Thank God you're on your toes."

It was straight ahead of them, hidden behind some dangling vegetation, appearing at first glance to be nothing more than darkness.

Immediately, the three of them headed toward the cave, brushing past the plants and hurrying inside.

The wave hit, like a liquid fist carrying the power of a million heavyweight champions delivering their best knockout punch ever— a force so devastating that the mountain seemed almost to groan on impact.

Inside the cave, soil dropped from between cracks in the rock, and was stirred up into a cloud, just before water came rushing inside. The sheer power of it knocked them off their feet. But they were spared the full fury of the wave as they were protected by the centuries-old natural barrier into which they had run for refuge.

When the force of the water reversed and began to recede, Ryan, Chad, and Mr. Bartlett were being pulled out with it. They had to grab hold of boulders or vines or whatever else was within reach.

It's still not over, Ryan thought. *When is it going to end? Are we all going to die together? Oh, Lord, how much longer can we hold out?*

Even athletic, muscular Chad, who could bench-press 250 pounds anytime anywhere, was becoming weary after facing that ordeal in the downed helicopter and the struggle to shore. Now this! He felt his own strength rapidly giving way.

Not yet, Lord, he prayed. *Not like this . . . please give us just a little more time!*

Andrew Bartlett was thinking along similar lines as he glanced at his sons, trying as they were to keep from being sucked out of the cave and back into the ocean which was waiting to claim all three of them.

Finally, the danger had passed.

As they were getting to their feet, Mr. Bartlett, breathing heavily, managed to say, "There may be another. We've got to see where this leads, get as far inland as possible."

"So many waves, Dad, one right after the other?" Chad asked, doubt in his voice. "Isn't that unusual? I always thought tidal waves hit once, maybe twice, and that was it."

"Unusual? Oh, it is, but not completely unheard of. Besides, worldwide conditions now are a little bizarre anyway. All at once, we're having a rash of earthquakes, volcanic eruptions, tidal waves, and a great deal more."

Ryan obviously wanted to speak but seemed a bit undecided, which was usual for him.

"What is it, son?" his father asked. "You have something on your mind. Spit it out."

"Dad," Ryan said, a frown on his forehead, "I was wondering if this could be that time of . . . turbulence around the world, just before . . . you know . . . the Rapture happens."

"It might be, son," his father admitted. "It might be indeed."

The possibility of that forced them all into silence for a moment.

"But we can't just stand here and wait for that to happen," Mr. Bartlett told them. "Because we might be wrong. People have guessed before, during one historical period or another, and they have been proven off the mark. Life has to go on. We've been spared yet again. Let's be grateful for that, and take anything else as it comes."

The cave was deep, but not totally dark. A small amount of light was filtering through cracks where much of the soil had washed away from between the rocks.

The cave led to a complicated and extensive tunnel system that was truly like an underground maze. But there was more than that which surprised them. The tunnels were unique in quite another way.

Wide . . .

Much wider than the three of them had seen before, except those that were man-made. These tunnels weren't as wide as those dug through mountains for the purpose of allowing vehicles to take a more direct route. But Ryan, Chad, and Andrew Bartlett could walk side by side and still not quite touch the tunnel to their left or their right.

"What we have here is remarkable," Mr. Bartlett commented. "I've never seen anything natural that was as mammoth as this."

The three Bartletts guessed that they must have walked at least two or three miles already. They didn't really know at all where they were heading, but they were convinced that going back the way they had come could mean yet another battle with another gigantic wave. This would continue to be a possibility until the ocean patterns returned to normal. And there was no way any of them had to determine that conditions were even close to that point.

The cave tunnels were very damp. But this wasn't all that surprising, since Oahu and the other islands were in a region that received much rainfall. Sometimes it was just a light shower called *pineapple rain*, one that people could walk through without difficulty. But on other occasions, the rain came down in fierce, typically tropical fashion.

"I wonder if anyone else has been through here," Ryan commented. "I don't see anything human at all."

"It gives the impression of being an ancient place, that's for sure," Mr. Bartlett replied. "And, you're right, it looks as though it hasn't been disturbed by anyone for a very long time."

Musty. A musty smell hung in the air.

They had smelled it before, in places of great age like the interior of the Great Pyramid on the outskirts of Cairo, Egypt.

Mother tried it that one time, Chad remembered fondly. *She wanted so much to prove to us how brave she was. But she just couldn't stand being inside that massive tomb, with four thousand years of death surrounding her. She got halfway through the tour and had to leave. Afterwards, she was concerned that we might be ashamed of her. Of course, we all did our best to tell her that nothing she did or didn't do would ever make us feel anything but love for her.*

As Ryan, Chad, and Mr. Bartlett turned a natural corner in the underground tunnel system, they came upon an astonishing sight and stopped suddenly in their tracks, gasping as they took it in.

The narrow tunnel system suddenly opened up into a huge cavern.

At the top, in the middle of the high rock ceiling, there was an opening which was about forty inches in diameter, and sunlight filtered through, casting beams of light throughout the cavern.

Heads tilted upward, Ryan, Chad, and Mr. Bartlett stood underneath, letting the warm light splash over them.

"It's so wonderful, Dad," Chad said. "It feels to me as though heaven is somehow shining through and we three are actually waiting for the Lord to call us, waiting for Him to—"

Just then Chad noticed something that, at first, they all had completely missed.

"Dad, Ryan, look!" Chad shouted, pointing excitedly at what it was that had caught his attention.

I can hardly believe what I'm seeing, Mr. Bartlett said to himself, his mouth dropping open in amazement.

In the rock walls, they now could see scores of carved out sections, some bigger than others. And inside each one, there seemed to be pieces of bone, or remains of some sort. But there wasn't enough left to be able to identify them.

The sections went from ground level to way above their heads!

"This is like the Roman catacombs!" Mr. Bartlett exclaimed. "It's unbelievable!"

"Where did all this come from?" Ryan asked.

"And why hasn't such a spot been discovered before now?" Chad wondered. "Lots of tourists come to Oahu each year, a million or more. You'd think that they'd have been over every inch of the island by now."

"The tidal waves, son," Mr. Bartlett suggested. "I doubt that there has ever been a series like what we've witnessed here over the past few hours. And who knows what's ahead? In addition, the eruptions from Diamond Head have created earthquake-like rumblings over the whole land mass."

"The rock and soil were loosened," Ryan said, connecting everything together in his mind, "and the waves washed them away. This tunnel system and, therefore, this cavern have been hidden for a long time!"

"I'd say that's about it," Mr. Bartlett agreed. "These excavations may be hundreds of years old."

"But why here? Why this way?" Ryan probed. "Hawaiians used to cremate their dead. Burials like this would have been very unusual."

"It may be something else that seems strange to us in our scientific world today," Mr. Bartlett started to say, rubbing his chin for a moment. "But, no, that's crazy."

"What were you going to say Dad?"

"It was too crazy, Chad. That's why I hesitated. I know you can handle anything I say, but this is just so much nonsense."

"Give us a clue."

"Those aren't human remains," Mr. Bartlett said.

"How do you know that, Dad?" Chad asked, with a touch of admiration and curiosity. "So little is left of the bodies. I mean, really, they're mostly bits and pieces of bone. The rest has turned to nothing more than dust."

"I'll say this much," his father replied. "This whole region must have been underwater at some point centuries ago."

"How can you tell?" Ryan asked.

"Look at the moss," Mr. Bartlett pointed to the clinging green growth on the sides of the cavern.

He walked over to one of the carved out places in the wall.

"And inside each one . . . look!" he said, excited, and a little like a teenager himself. "Here's something else."

They joined him.

"The bodies once were anchored to the rock by tough underwater vines or possibly man-made ropes."

Ryan and Chad looked closely at what their father was pointing out. On both sides of each body were two holes in the rock about an inch and a half apart. A vine or rope or something else had been draped around the remains and slipped into one hole and out the other, then tied into a strong knot. Over the centuries, most of what tied them down had rotted away, but probably not before the water receded and left the interior of the cavern ultimately quite dry.

"Dad!" Chad said excitedly. "This is amazing!"

"It is that," Mr. Bartlett agreed, "and more besides, Chad. Since they're not human, what in the world are they?"

Andrew Bartlett looked closer at the remains in front of him.

"I wish more of their bone structure had been preserved. All I see now are fragments. But I guess anything better, well, that's too much to ask for, under the circumstances."

They spent the next few minutes examining as much of the cavern as possible.

"I guess there's nothing else," Mr. Bartlett said. "While it's still light, let's head on and see if we can find a way out!"

In their haste, Ryan brushed against an outjutting small section of rock in the wall of the cavern. He jumped aside as the rock fell to the ground.

Ryan was about to go past when he glanced at where the rock had been.

A little alcove.

"Dad! Chad!" he said, his voice briefly echoing in the cavern. "I've found something. Come here!"

He had indeed.

"A parchment," his father said as he carefully reached in and pulled out the rolled-up piece of very brittle, paper-like substance.

"It seems to have been kept here, waterproof, for a long time," Ryan observed. "What do you think, Dad?"

"I think you're right, son," Mr. Bartlett said. "It could be a papyrus scroll. I don't dare try to unroll it, to see what the contents are. Professionals will have to do that. We need to be extremely careful with this if we take it with us.

"I just hope we aren't confronted by any more natural calamities. This won't hold up at all well, you know. Be on the lookout for a hollow piece of wood, so that we can put the scroll inside, to give it at least a little protection until it can be examined properly."

"The papyrus, or whatever it is, is so thin," Chad pointed out. "I can just make out strange letters that are showing through. They look like some kind of ancient writing."

"They sure do," Mr. Bartlett agreed, after examining them himself. "If it weren't so dangerous, I could almost start to like the situation we've gotten ourselves into this time. Fascinating!"

His two sons agreed. All three of them had been interested in archaeology for a long time.

"It's like being a detective," Ryan had said a couple of years earlier, "except that you hunt for ruins, not criminals."

On a trip to Brazil, they had stumbled upon some ruins that belonged not to the Mayans, Aztecs, or Incas but to an altogether different group of ancient peoples.

There was nothing supernatural or otherworldly about that discovery. When thousands of years of history were involved, it was little wonder that such a group had previously slipped through the cracks and gone unnoticed.

"Remember Brazil?" Ryan asked out loud.

"I do," Mr. Bartlett replied.

"Me, too," Chad added. "That was incredible!"

"This may be just as important," Ryan suggested.

He looked around once again at the cavern.

"I wonder who used this place centuries ago," he mused. "Will we ever know?"

"The scroll may contain some of the answers," his father said. "In the meantime, let's get out of here and back above ground."

 **Eleven**

The tunnel system continued on and on. All three Bartletts were getting tired. And they had no idea of when they would make it back to the surface.

Chad was hungry.

"Man, I could use some prime beef right now," he said. "I can see it sizzling on the grill!"

"That sounds good," Ryan admitted. "But I'll have some with a special brown sauce on top."

"You and your sauces! Just the pure beef for this dude."

Their father had continued ahead of them as they paused for a moment.

"Do you think we'll have as much energy as Dad does when we're his age?" Chad said.

"Probably," said Ryan. "We know his secret."

"He doesn't smoke," Ryan reminded his brother. "That's one big thing in his favor, Chad. And neither do we."

"You said it! Getting that stuff into your body can do nothing but bad things to it."

Both boys had learned at an early age that alcohol and tobacco were drugs. And their Dad had taught them to stay clear of all drugs except medicines taken as part of a doctor's treatment.

"Every so often, somebody approaches me at the gym," Chad admitted. "I seem like an ideal candidate, I suppose. They've got some steroids. They'll sell the lot to me cheap. They tempt me by saying that I can pump up even more than I am already."

"Often?" Ryan asked. "Does that happen really often?"

"Once a month, maybe. It's appealing to anyone who doesn't know the truth about that stuff. Sure, you can look great for a while. But, years later, your brain is eaten away by steroids, and your nervous system is destroyed. You die twenty years sooner than you should!"

They suddenly realized they couldn't see their father or hear him.

"Awful quiet ahead of us," Ryan said, almost afraid of going ahead for the moment, to face whatever it was that might be there, or might not be there.

"We were so wrapped up in chattering between ourselves that we lost track of things," Chad replied. "Let's hustle now!"

Ryan and Chad hurried ahead to find their father. But instead they found something else. A primitive flight of stairs that had been notched into the wall! Leading to nowhere! It came right smack up against solid rock

"How weird!" Ryan exclaimed. "Those steps lead to the ceiling, so what? What good does that do?"

They had an answer soon enough. Something moving. In the ceiling. A slab of stone being pushed aside noisily.

Sunlight was now shining through, so brightly in fact that they had to cover their eyes at first. A familiar voice called down, "Hey, guys, hurry on up! We're out of here!"

As their eyes adjusted to the sudden light, after hours of walking in hardly no light at all, they saw Andrew Bartlett poke his head down through an irregular-shaped hole in the rock ceiling of that tunnel.

"You have to see this," he shouted. "Hurry, please. This is so beautiful I think we could be very close to the Rapture right now!"

The Rapture.

That was the prophesied event involving the return of Jesus Christ to Earth, and His gathering together of all redeemed Christians around the world, and their journey with Him back to heaven.

"Oh, Dad, it could be!" Ryan said in wonderment. "It really could."

"The earthquakes, the famine, all the rest," Mr. Bartlett added. "It's all there in the Bible. And many of those happenings *have* been occurring lately.

"Yet it may not be that at all, guys. We just have to be alert, to be ready if it should come while you and I are still alive."

Nevertheless, what was happening in the sky indeed was astonishing, perhaps a hint of the Rapture to come, perhaps not. The sky had turned shades of blue and purple plus turquoise.

"I wonder who else can see what we're seeing," Mr. Bartlett said. "It might be the whole world! Think of that! Wouldn't that be something, I mean, that it wasn't confined just to this area but was global!"

And then the celestial display was over. As quickly as it had begun.

"I wonder what caused that," Chad remarked.

"I don't know," Mr. Bartlett said. "But I'll say this, the three of us made a classic mistake just now."

"How do you mean that?" Chad asked.

"The Rapture will take all of us by surprise if we're alive when it occurs. You, Ryan, might be at your computer. Yes, that could be it . . . in the middle of typing a sentence."

He snapped his fingers.

"Just like that, you'll be gone."

He turned to Chad.

"And you, son, could be lifting weights."

He snapped his finger once more.

"You'll be gone, too, Chad. Think of it! In the twinkling of an eye, as the Bible says. Those barbells of yours will drop right to the floor because you won't have even a few seconds to put them down before . . . before you're taken up to heaven."

They looked at one another, their minds swirling with the reality of that promise from the Bible.

"Signs and wonders, Dad," Ryan reminded him. "Is that a possibility here?"

"I don't know but when we get back home, we'll study the Bible to see what it says about that."

# Twelve

Another unexpected encounter! They had walked some distance from where they had come out of the cave tunnels.

Ryan observed that the mountains ahead seemed far taller than any others they had spotted before then.

"You're right, son," Mr. Bartlett said. "And I don't remember seeing them on any of our other trips to this island."

"You think we're the first ones in years to come this way?" Chad asked, fascinated by the thought.

"It's entirely possible," his father replied. "I don't see any evidence to the contrary, do you?"

Ryan and Chad had to agree that it seemed no one else had been through that way anytime recently.

A narrow pass.

They approached it and walked through cautiously, having no idea of what would confront them, once they reached the other side.

A valley. An extraordinary valley that seemed totally unspoiled!

They were in an area of the densest jungle-like growth any of them had ever seen on Oahu. The clearing in which they stood was quite small. The vines and flowers and bushes and other vegetation were packed closely together in front of them, so much so that they wished they had a machete to hack away some of it.

"This is like a hidden valley," Mr. Bartlett observed as he saw the mist-covered mountain peaks rising up on every side. "I doubt that anybody can see it from the air because of the thick overhang of trees. I wonder if anyone else has ever been here?"

"So peaceful," Ryan said, listening to a bird singing, fascinated by the sound. "Oh, Dad, it's like a canary but different. I've never heard any bird sing as beautifully as whatever that one is."

"I hear it, and you're right, son," Mr. Bartlett said. "And the sweet smelling flowers are nice, too. Breathe deeply and take in this wonderful combination of scents. You may never come across them again."

The three stood quietly then, breathing in the air, enjoying the sweet fragrance of the flowers.

They were interrupted by the sound of a child.

A child was laughing.

"It's coming from over there," Ryan said, pointing at a large old twisted, thick-trunked tree to his left. "Behind that tree . . . I think."

They walked together to it, and around the side.

Little Benny! The little boy looked up at them, smiling, as he was feeding a cute little monkey perched on his left shoulder.

"The man said I would be safe here," he told them, in his squeaky voice. "Did he tell you the same thing?"

So isolated, with no threats from the outside world, with fruits to eat, and a roof of stars over their heads . . .

They were in that valley the rest of the day and through the night, enjoying its beauty, its calm. Benny, in his simple, childlike way, told them the remarkable story of how he had come to the valley. A tall, thin stranger had pulled him from the ocean and led him around the cove, up a mountain trail, and through that narrow pass into the valley.

"I fed squirrels and monkeys," he said, his eyes wide, shining with memories of the experience, as he tried to pronounce another word that wasn't so easy for him. "And a little mon . . . mon . . ."

"Mongoose," Chad offered.

"Mon . . . mongoose," the boy repeated.

"Those animals were brought here to the Hawaiian Islands many years ago to get rid of the snakes," Ryan added. "They've been the best animal friends for everyone living out here."

"Yeah . . . he said that, too, the man told me just what you said."

"Where is he now?" Mr. Bartlett asked, fascinated by what Benny might be suggesting.

"He went away," Benny replied simply.

"Where, son?" Mr. Bartlett pressed him gently. "Do you know where?"

"Up."

"Up?"

"There!"

Benny pointed toward the sky.

"Like Superman?" Ryan asked.

"Like an angel . . . wings . . . he had wings," the little boy remarked with such matter-of-factness that no one questioned his sincerity.

Ryan, Chad, and their father glanced at one another, uncertain how to respond.

"Dad?" Ryan said.

"Yes, son?"

"We've talked about miracles a lot. Could we be in the midst of a whole bunch of them happening?"

Mr. Bartlett nodded as he said, "That indeed could be the case. Look at the very fact that we're all here alive after what's been happening! The chances of that being the case from a medical or scientific viewpoint are so slim that they almost don't exist at all.

"Volcanic eruptions and tidal waves, then being trapped underwater in a helicopter—and we don't have any injuries either, except maybe a few scratches and bruises."

"Dad?" It was Chad's turn this time. But he seemed a little uncertain, not used to talking about miracles.

"I wonder if maybe we've seen miracles other times before now, without realizing it," he went on. "We could have died when we were kidnapped by those guys from the Forbidden River drug cartel. Or when the *S. S. Oceanic* sank. And those mobsters could have killed us when we stumbled onto the Frankenstein Project.

"The list goes on and on, Dad. One incident after another. But then why was Mom taken? Why couldn't that have been another miracle, to have her survive? Why has it been us but not Mom?"

Andrew Bartlett had no neat, tying-everything-together answer to give to them.

"We have to remember that *no* can be an answer to prayer as much as *yes*. Though God can display miracles whenever He wants, He often decides not to do that. We may not understand why, but we have to accept it.

"What we have to remember," he did say, "is that she's happy now. She's at peace, no more pain for her. She's never going to die again. And she's walking with the angels."

Tears started down his cheeks.

"Don't cry," Benny said.

"We loved her so much," Mr. Bartlett replied.

"The stranger told me to tell you somethin'."

"He knows about us?" Chad asked.

"He said he does," Benny told him. "He said your mom is real happy in heaven. And there's someone else there you know . . ."

Ryan, Chad, and Mr. Bartlett could not speak. They sat on the fresh, soft grass not understanding what was happening.

"A man . . . " Benny remembered, struggling with the words that he had heard spoken to him just once. "A man . . . I . . . I . . . his name . . . "

"Take it easy," Ryan said softly. "It's all right. The name doesn't matter."

"It does . . . it does!" Benny blurted out. "I just can't say it. I can't. I forgot, I forgot!"

Benny acted as though he was ashamed of himself. Mr. Bartlett put his arms around the boy.

"Don't get upset," he said. "Soon there'll be another miracle. Soon you'll be back with your own parents."

"But the stranger wanted me to tell you this. He really did. He said that it meant a lot, that it was all he would ask . . . It was about someone who had been a mean man, a man who did bad things."

"Like kill people?" Ryan put in abruptly, surprised at himself, a strange sensation of gathering awareness going up and down his back, like an icicle that sent chills throughout his body.

"Yeah . . . yeah!" Benny said. "He killed people. He—." Benny paused, trying hard to remember everything the stranger had said.

The three Bartletts seemed frozen where they sat, able now to understand more of what Benny was talking about but not able, yet, to believe. But yet they knew that there was no way, no way at all that this little boy, a stranger himself, could have known.

"Was the man's name Giovanni?" Mr. Bartlett asked finally, though barely able to speak. "Was it . . . Paul Giovanni?"

Benny nodded with great enthusiasm as soon as he heard this, an eager smile lighting up his very young face.

"That's it! That's what he told me. He said the mean man isn't the same anymore . . . he changed. And now he's with your mama and the angels in heaven!"

Thirteen

It's too much, Lord. You're asking too much of me this time, Ryan prayed. *I'm not superhuman. I don't have special powers. I can't cope with the idea that a gangster is in heaven with my mother!*

In the four years since his mother's death, Ryan had made real strides in coping with not having her near him, not seeing her beautiful smile, and not hearing her familiar voice. But . . . this message little Benny had just given them was hard to take.

Paul Giovanni had died only a short while after accepting Jesus Christ as his Savior. And now he was in heaven.

How was it, Ryan wondered, *that God would allow such an individual to share in all the glories of heaven with his mother and other longtime faithful Christians?*

That central question—How?—was not new to Ryan, but he thought he had dealt with it. Obviously he had only stored it on some kind of mental "back burner," until it absolutely could not be avoided.

Like now . . .

That night, Ryan, Chad, Mr. Bartlett, and little Benny slept outdoors, under the clear sky. No other choice was available to them. They had nothing with them but the now-ragged clothes they were wearing.

Ryan *tried* to sleep, but couldn't.

He had camped out more than once over the years in a tent or a sleeping bag, but now there were none of these things.

On those other occasions Ryan had found that he could sleep just about anywhere. Yet, here, in the middle of a kind of earthly paradise, after two days of calamity, he couldn't sleep at all.

Ryan finally got up, as quietly as he could manage. After surveying the scene, now bathed in moonlight, he spotted a little path through the dense, multi-colored vegetation. And he decided to walk a bit, being careful not to wander very far or lose track of his location.

Despite all the damage caused by the various natural disasters that had occurred over the past twenty-four hours, birds continued to sing, even at night, and there were still sweet scents in the air.

Before long, Ryan found a large tree and sat down underneath it. The grass was thick and he leaned back and closed his eyes, still thinking about what little Benny had said.

"Little changes, son," a voice said.

Ryan sat up. Had he been asleep? Was he dreaming?

He looked around. A tall, thin man was standing half in shadow, half in moonlight. He was dressed in a bright yellow shirt and dark brown shorts.

"Are you the one who spoke to Benny?" Ryan asked.

"I am indeed," the man said. "What can I do for you, Ryan Bartlett?"

"How come you know my name?"

"There is a great deal that I know."

"Who are you, really?" Ryan asked, annoyed by the fact that the man seemed almost to be toying with him.

"That should not matter."

"It does," Ryan protested. "How can you know that Paul Giovanni is in heaven with my mother?"

"Your mother was a believer?"

"Yes, of course."

"This man of whom you speak changed. He became one as well."

"Yes but—!" Ryan started to shout.

"So the Bible says that murderers cannot be admitted to heaven? Tell me, is that what you mean to say?"

"I'm not saying that."

"What are you saying then?"

Ryan wasn't sure. He knew emotion had taken over. He tried to calm down, to deal with the situation intelligently.

"Won't you tell me who you are, sir?" he asked, a note of pleading in his voice.

"No, Ryan Bartlett, I will not."

Ryan's shoulders drooped.

"I will show you, son," the stranger said, smiling quite broadly. "But close your eyes just for a moment. Will you do that one thing for me?"

Ryan nodded and closed his eyes. A few seconds later, he opened them again.

The stranger was gone.

"Where are you?" Ryan asked, raising his voice quite a bit.

That was when he turned toward the sky. That was when he saw something incredibly beautiful, a being of light and sparkle, a being of blue-and-green-and-yellow.

"You asked me who I am," a voice said, a strong and beautiful and deep voice unlike any Ryan had heard before.

Ryan stood motionless, listening to every word.

"I am as I am now," the voice continued, "and you must know that what I said about Paul Giovanni is true."

Then, for an instant, Ryan saw Paul Giovanni. He saw his mother. The two of them seemed so happy as they walked with others on a street of shiny pure gold. Beings like the one the stranger had become were gathered all around his mother and Paul Giovanni.

And music. Music unlike any Ryan had ever heard before.

He fell to the ground, fell to the soft grass, his eyes closing.

In the background, words seemed to be coming to him as though from across eternity, words that sounded like, "Please forgive this man, my beloved Ryan. Forgive him as I have. Will you do that for me, son?"

Ryan lost consciousness, overwhelmed, but oddly at peace with the sound of his mother's voice welcome in his ears.

"Ryan! Ryan! Why did you wonder off like that?"
The voice was his father's.

Completely asleep at last, Ryan had been resting on nature's mattress of thick grass under a large tree.

"We were frantic, Ryan. What happened, son?"

He opened his eyes slowly, saw his father and Chad standing over him, and Benny nearby.

"I'm sorry," he said sheepishly. "I just wanted to stretch my legs, clear my head."

"What happened?" Chad asked. "You were mumbling in your sleep."

Ryan told them.

"The same man," Benny said, suddenly excited by what he heard. "The same stranger!"

"Or the same dream," Mr. Bartlett commented. He hated to be contrary, but he was trying to be as realistic as he knew how, knowing that wishful thinking could be a part of such encounters.

"But . . . Dad . . . " Ryan protested, "you believe in angels as much as Chad and I do!"

"That's right, but this is so strange."

"And so beautiful, Dad. Besides, how would Benny here have known what none of us had ever told him? How could he have guessed what happened to Mom?"

Mr. Bartlett paused. He had to admit that Ryan made sense in a situation that had seemed at first to make no sense at all.

"This could be a strange and wonderful place of miracles, Dad," Ryan said, getting to his feet and looking around at the beautiful valley. "I think that cave is part of it. That scroll might tell us more when we can get an expert to tell us what it says."

"A place of miracles . . . " Mr. Bartlett repeated those words, as though wishing his son had indeed spoken what was true.

He cleared his throat, obviously to say something else that would not come easily.

"I saw him, too," he acknowledged at last to the three of them. "Last night . . . I . . . I couldn't sleep either. So I got up and apparently walked in another direction. And there he was, so kind, so understanding, so eager for me to be at peace. I saw him change. I saw him become so beautiful that I don't have the words to describe how he looked."

"You?" Ryan said, astonished.

"And me," Chad said, adding his confession to the others and feeling relieved because there was no need to keep what had occurred a secret.

"Could all of us be imagining things?" Ryan asked. "Is that really likely, Dad?"

"I don't know, son, I just don't. What we've experienced here has been kind and good and is pointing our minds and hearts and souls to what the Lord has been asking of us. So I find it hard to believe that any of this is counterfeit or some form of false belief on our part. But we can't be sure. And we mustn't fall into the trap of expecting miracles on demand."

He sighed wistfully.

"We may never know the truth," Mr. Bartlett said. "We can only take with us the fact that we have survived and be thankful for that."

 # Fourteen

They left that isolated spot a short while later. And it was with some reluctance that they did this, since they all felt so serene there, and peaceful. The ever-present music of the birds was so comforting, and the fragrant scents of tropical plants so sweet in the warm, gentle breezes of that special valley!

After embracing one another amidst cleansing tears, Ryan, Chad, Mr. Bartlett, and Benny finally managed to get to a major highway. They hoped that traffic was beginning to move again and that soon someone would give them a ride.

When an Army truck came along within an hour or so, they all rejoiced as it slowed in front of them, then stopped. The driver asked if he could help. In an instant his eyes widened as he saw Mr. Bartlett.

"Are you Andrew Bartlett, the President's National Security Advisor?" he added.

"I am," Mr. Bartlett replied. "Tell me, sergeant, what is it like over at Honolulu?"

"Not good at all, sir," the driver, a sergeant named Robert Ettinger, told him. "There's lots of chaos and disorder even now, three days later. Sure, we're gradually getting everything calmed down. But what you'll see in the city isn't going to be pretty or encouraging."

"Encouraging? About what?"

"Human nature, sir."

"We're Christians, sergeant. The Bible is pretty straight talking about human behavior. I doubt that there is anything in this world that could surprise me or my two sons!"

After they were on their way, Ettinger noticed the scroll Mr. Bartlett carried.

"Where did you find that, sir?" he asked.

"In a cave a few miles from here."

"It looks ancient."

"It probably is."

A minute or two passed, without anyone speaking.

"Sir," the sergeant said, changing the subject, "did you hear about the dolphins?"

"What about them?" Mr. Bartlett asked.

"Their behavior, I mean."

"Any different than usual?"

"I wouldn't say different, sir, just, well, may I tell you?" Ettinger asked hesitantly.

"Fine, go ahead."

"People were acting like crazed cattle or suicidal lemmings, running in every direction, trying to stay ahead of the invading lava, but often running headlong into their own destruction instead," the sergeant told them, his body trembling with awful memories.

"It was a terrible sight, sir—people on fire, running into the ocean. Several were attacked by sharks. But then the miracle happened."

"Dolphins came and helped," Ryan put in, embarrassed that he had interrupted Ettinger.

"How did you know?"

"Well, it's a long story," Ryan said, "but they helped us survive, too. Go on, sergeant."

"Having hundreds of dolphins fight off a dozen or so sharks was an incredible sight in itself. But the greatest was yet to come.

"The dolphins stayed.

"They stayed in and around the area of the greatest calamities, from near Diamond Head, west to Pearl Harbor.

"Thousands of them, we figure," the sergeant said. "The hundreds that had bested the sharks were a fraction of the vast numbers that joined them over a period of hours. They were waiting to keep other sharks away, to help however they could, probably to keep panic-stricken tourists and others from drowning."

"It sounds a bit fanciful, sergeant," Mr. Bartlett told him, though not as disbelieving as he pretended to be.

"I would have agreed with you except that I saw it myself. They'd disperse just before another tidal wave hit, then they'd be back, their numbers larger, not smaller."

"Would you like to hear about our experiences, sergeant, the ones that my son hinted about a few moments ago?" Mr. Bartlett said, with barely controlled excitement in his voice.

"I sure would, sir," Ettinger assured him. "Were they anything like what I've just said?"

"You decide."

The sergeant listened.

When Mr. Bartlett had finished, Ettinger fell briefly silent, stunned by the combination of what he himself had seen, and, now, what the Bartletts also had experienced.

"Those mammals really are special, aren't they?" he said finally.

"It's apparent that they are," Mr. Bartlett agreed. "It's apparent that God has given them a purpose in this world."

"To be helpful to human beings?" the sergeant asked.

"I just don't know what else is available to

explain incident after incident over a period of at least fifty years. And there were some scattered reports even before World War II."

"Dad?" Ryan put in.

"What is it, son?"

"Should we question, should we wonder, should we poke and pry so much, or just accept the blessing?"

Mr. Bartlett rubbed his chin for a moment, realizing that his son had made a strong point.

"You're right," he replied. "We thank the Lord, we accept in faith, and we go on from there."

Their minds were taken off dolphins and a great deal else when they approached the outskirts of Honolulu and saw the living nightmare that had not as yet ended.

Buildings had toppled, and very little of the wreckage had been cleaned up. Huge sections of lava remained, some beginning the slow process of hardening, others still steaming. The normally bustling International Marketplace had simply ceased to exist. The booths and stores within that area were buried after the taller buildings on either side had collapsed onto them.

Every hotel had damage, with glass fragments all over the sidewalk and the street. All the bodies had been removed by now, but little else had been cleared away.

The frames of burned automobiles were among the wreckage that still remained. Some had crashed into store windows along the shopping area. Others had plowed into telephone poles and some into fire hydrants, not to mention those that had collided with other cars and trucks.

"It looked like a scene out of hell two days ago," Sergeant Ettinger told them, "all the fires . . . people running in fear and pain. Now it just seems like the bombed out remnants of a city in some distant wartime."

"Nearly deserted now," Mr. Bartlett observed, "and kind of eerie. Just four days ago, this place had almost too much activity."

"That's right, sir. Only personnel from Pearl Harbor are allowed in. A military barricade has been established around the city."

They drove through to the huge Ala Moana Shopping Center not far from the Honolulu waterfront area.

"We've made this the civilian center," Ettinger remarked. "It wasn't damaged by the tidal waves. They were more concentrated near the center of Waikiki and on the wind-ward side of Oahu. And it wasn't damaged by the eruptions themselves either, since the lava flow stopped a few blocks away."

They got out of the truck after pulling into the parking garage. Military vehicles took up nearly every space.

"Some electrical power has been restored," the sergeant told them as they walked up a flight of stairs. "There are plenty of restaurants here, as well as clothing stores, and medical supplies in the pharmacy . . . most of what we need on a daily basis, at least for the short term . . . "

"Mama! Daddy!" Benny's cry interrupted the sergeant as they entered the main level of the mall.

The little boy had spotted his parents in a group gathered at a center section of the mall. They were eating some French fries.

Benny rushed up to the relieved couple, and the three hugged and hugged.

A few moments later, as the Bartletts introduced themselves, Diamond Head erupted again!

 **Fifteen**

Lights went out. People were screaming. Panic started to take hold. Just at that moment, no other military personnel were in the area. Realizing what was required of him, Sergeant Ettinger gulped nervously a couple of times and then stepped forward, holding a large beamed flashlight that had been dangling from his belt.

"We're safe," he said as loud, as forcefully as possible. "The lava flow is unlikely to reach any farther this time than it did before."

Ettinger took charge with convincing authority, calming down the crowd as much as he could. And he succeeded better than he expected, in part simply by being someone wearing a uniform who seemed to know pretty much what he was doing.

That eruption turned out to be a short one, a fluke of sorts. But an earth tremor along with it had momentarily knocked out one outlying power station that had been somehow spared during the earlier eruptions and tidal waves.

But the molten rock didn't go far this time, and no additional lives were lost as a result.

In minutes, other soldiers were being rushed in throughout the shopping center, with better portable lighting. Within an hour, circuits were rerouted and power was restored to Ala Moana.

"We have only the clothes we're wearing, Dad," Chad remarked, without embarrassment, but drawing the older Bartlett's attention to their torn clothing.

"For you, that's not a problem," Ryan quipped. "You don't *need* a shirt to cover up a puny little chest."

"Work out more when we get back to the mainland."

"Easy to say for a hunk like you. Me? Hey, I've tried before, lots of times. Nothing—."

His words were shut off by a rumbling sound.

Suddenly that huge structure shook, like an ancient dinosaur that had been mortally wounded.

Another tidal wave?

Not this time!

It was something that would prove to be at least as dangerous. The tormented ground on which they stood, stressed as it had been by volcanic turmoil, battered by giant walls of water, was no longer going to be as tolerant as before.

The earth rebelled. It said, in effect, no more.

And that was when an earthquake, measuring 6.8 on the Richter Scale, tore up the Hawaiian island of Oahu, as it wrote the final devastating chapter for what later would be called Disaster Island!

Rubble. People moaning.

It's like that time our plane crashed just outside Washington, D.C., Ryan recalled, as he remained unmoving, aware that he could aggravate any injuries he might have sustained if he tried to get to his feet too quickly. *Only this is so much worse, with many more people involved!*

How many hours have we been unconscious? Chad asked of himself, as he saw his brother stirring beside him. *Is there daylight outside now? Or is it nighttime instead?*

So dark, Ettinger thought, remembering a time during military boot camp training when he became momentarily panicked by a similar enveloping darkness. *That was just playacting, however real it was meant to seem. There is no make-believe this time!*

There were so many strange noises . . . gasps and shrieks and groans . . . breathing that was uneven, like snoring but far more serious, probably meaning that the sufferers were very close to death.

And someone talking in the darkness, someone praying.

"Dear Lord, see us through this valley of the shadow of Your enemy, for it was by Satan that death was visited upon this world."

And nearby, someone else began to sing the old hymn *Abide with Me:*

> *. . . The darkness deepens,*
> *Lord, with me abide!*
> *When other helpers fail, and comforts flee,*
> *Help of the helpless . . .*

The voice stopped before the verse was finished, silenced for whatever reason.

Ryan finally tried to move but couldn't. He was pinned down by the wreckage. He knew that straining himself could result in untold injury, probably worse than any he had sustained thus far.

Total darkness. No light existed anywhere. Only those sounds could be heard.

Ryan started to hallucinate, talking out of his head. The pain was messing up his mind. Fear and the confusion of being surrounded by such blackness, all mixed together to take away his sense of time and place.

Dad! he thought he said, but couldn't be certain that it was a word that reached his lips from his mind or just remained there, unspoken after all.

He could move his hands, just his hands, and he clasped them tightly together.

Jesus, Jesus, he spoke but only to himself, and yet beyond himself, beyond that crumpled building, through the air to heaven itself. *Tell Mom it may not be long, Lord. Please tell her that.*

Other sounds.

Movement.

A voice.

Voices.

Far away.

Down a long tunnel, echoing.

Now closer.

So much closer.

And light.

From the distance.

Nearer.

Light in a beam, piercing the blackness.

Vague outlines.

Twisted concrete.

Metal girders pointing upward.

And a face, a soldier's face, close to his own, words whispered in his ear, "It'll be all right, son. Be still."

Ryan smiled.

Thank you, Lord . . .

 # Epilogue

Ryan, Chad, and Andrew Bartlett were rescued from the wreckage, as were little Benny and his parents. But Sergeant Ettinger did not make it.

"Oh, Dad," Ryan said as they were being flown by helicopter to Pearl Harbor. "He was so fine, doing his best to help so many people. And now he's gone."

"Ettinger?" the pilot asked above the noise of the helicopter. "You're talking about him?"

"We are," Mr. Bartlett told him.

"I don't think you'll have to worry about where he will be spending eternity, sir."

"Why do you say that?"

"Ettinger was my best friend. He led me to Christ a few months ago."

The three Bartletts glanced at one another. Somehow they weren't surprised.

Below them, the destruction of the island was apparent even at night.

"It will be a very long time before this island recovers," the pilot went on to say. "I don't know if tourism will ever get back to what it was."

Little fires could be seen, smoke arising from ruins that continued to smolder.

"Dad! The scroll!" Ryan blurted out, suddenly remembering it.

Mr. Bartlett realized that he, like his sons, had forgotten all about it.

"We'll never know what it had to tell us," he said sadly.

"May I ask what you're talking about, sir?" the pilot put in.

Mr. Bartlett told him what they had encountered in the cave tunnels.

"You'll find all sorts of legends about dolphins in Hawaii," the pilot said. "I remember hearing one about how the natives hundreds of years ago started a burial place for them."

"Like Africa's elephant burial ground," Ryan added, "a place where they go to die."

"That seems to be it," the pilot agreed. "For centuries, that was where the dolphins went. They seemed to *know* that such a place had been started for them. They repaid the natives by protecting them from sharks."

"The scroll could have told us so much," Chad thought out loud. "What a shame!"

"I think we know all that is important," his father said. "What matters is that you, Ryan, and I are together and Benny is back with his family."

As the wreckage was being cleared away from where the Ala Moana Shopping Center once stood, a soldier found a battered scroll. Thinking it to be nothing more than a piece of advertising, he crumpled it up and threw it into a trash can, the contents of which would be burned minutes later . . .

DON'T MISS THESE OTHER BARTLETT BROTHER ADVENTURES:

Sudden Fear

When Ryan Bartlett accidently intercepts a computer message, he and his brother are stalked by terrorists, who plan to destroy a nuclear power plant. (ISBN 0–8499–3301–3)

Terror Cruise

The Bartlett family embarks on a Caribbean cruise that is supposed to be a time of rest and relaxation, but instead becomes a journey into terror. (ISBN 0–8499–3302–1)

The Frankenstein Project

While visiting a friend in the hospital, Ryan and Chad Bartlett come face to face with secret scientific experiments and mysterious children. (ISBN 0–8499–3303–X)

Forbidden River

The brothers find themselves in the midst of the war on drugs, with corruption and danger stretching from South America's Forbidden River to the U.S. Congress. (ISBN 0–8499–3304–8)

Nightmare at Skull Junction

A fun motorcycle ride in the desert turns into a nightmare for the Bartlett Brothers when they discover a plot to wipe out an entire Indian tribe.

(ISBN 0–8499–3361–7)

ABOUT THE AUTHOR

Award-winning author Roger Elwood is well known for his suspense-filled stories for both youth and adult readers. His twenty-six years of editing and writing experience include stories in *Today's Youth* and *Teen Life* magazines and a number of best-selling novels for Scholastic Book Clubs and Weekly Reader Book Clubs. He has also had titles featured by Junior Literary Guild and Science Fiction Book Club. Among his most outstanding adult books is *Angelwalk*, a winner of the Angel Award from Religion in Media.